The S...
MAT o...

JOAN AIKEN

Illustrated by
Caroline Crossland

RED FOX

A Red Fox Book

Published by Random House Chldren's Books
20 Vauxhall Bridge Road, London SW1V 2SA

A division of The Random House Group Ltd.
London Melbourne Sydney Auckland
Johannesburg and agencies throughout the world

1 3 5 7 9 10 8 6 4 2

First published in Great Britain by Red Fox 2001

Printed in Denmark by Norhaven A/S

THE RANDOM HOUSE GROUP Limited Reg.No.954009
www.randomhouse.co.uk

ISBN OO99411377

CHAPTER ONE

As I jogged towards the door of home I could hear the phone ringing inside the house, and I knew at once that it would be my Aunt Lal. I knew because I'd had a dream about her last night and when that happened it nearly always turned out that she had been dreaming about me. I opened the door, dropped my football boots on the mat and ran to the phone. But Mum had got there first.

'Yes, he is, Lally,' she was saying. 'Out playing in a match, yes; I should think he could – I'll ask him when he comes in – Oh!' she said, turning and seeing me, 'There you are, Ned. Aunt Lal wants to speak to you – '

She passed me the phone.

'I dreamed about you last night,' said the voice of Mum's sister.

'I know. I had the same dream.'

'In the book shop?'

'Yes, with the two little boys.'

It had been my Uncle Adam's book shop, which is on a sharp-angled corner site in the harbour town of St Boan. Antique bits and pieces, which the shop also sold, were displayed at the front, inside the window, and the books were at the back on three sets of shelves shaped like slices of pie. Uncle Adam has a stepladder, so that customers can reach the top shelves. In the dream Aunt Lal had been sitting

at the desk and I was up on the ladder
looking for some wonderful book which
I was certain would be there, when
these two little characters came
toddling into the shop. They could not
have been more than about three years
old, and were twins. I knew that,
although they were not much alike.
One of them had a tendency to go on
all fours. The other one led him along
on a lead. They had untidy brown
curls and freckled noses, and wore
queer little rusty black suits with white
Peter Pan collars.

The upright one was singing as they
came into the shop:
'Oh what adorable music we made,
As we danced through the town in the
Pilchard Parade.'
I knew the song of course, it's
famous, though his scrawny little
piping voice didn't do it much justice.

Then the singing twin stopped

singing and asked, 'Have you got our music book for us, with our song in it?' And Aunt Lal said, 'No I haven't, but Ned has it for you.'

Then I woke up.

'Do you know who those boys are?' said Aunt Lal over the phone.

'No idea.'

'They are the lost Pernel twins.'

The name was vaguely familiar, though I didn't pick up the link at first.

'Do you want me to help find them?' I said cautiously.

When Aunt Lal calls up it is often about some problem. She and I have a knack of helping each other sometimes, because of this shared-dream thing; we can come up with useful answers for each other's questions. But there was a football match tomorrow, our school against St Pardon; I had just got into the team. I didn't want to be away from home just then.

'No,' said Aunt Lal, 'the twins were lost a hundred years ago and they've been found, and that's what has led to a lot of trouble in the town. I'd very much like you to come over to St Boan, Neddy – I think you might be useful...'

'Could it possibly wait a day, Aunt Lal?'

'Better not. I think things might turn nasty...'

My heart sank. I knew that I ought to go. But how could I explain to Mike Pengelly, the team captain?

At that moment there came a knock at the door. And it was Mike.

'Hold on a tick, Aunt Lal – I'll just see what Mike wants.'

It was to say that tomorrow's match was postponed.

'There's a terrible weather forecast,' said Mike. 'Blizzard and three inches of snow.'

'Snow? In Cornwall? In March?'

Easter was close at hand, gardens were ablaze with daffodils.

'That's what they say,' said Mike. 'Fifty-mile-an-hour gales and a fifty-degree drop in temperature. I'd not plan any fishing trip in the next few days, young Ned. And the match is put off till tomorrow week. So long, see you.'

Off he went. So I told Aunt Lal I could come over and stay for a couple of nights.

'Oh dear,' said Mum. 'Is this a good time for you to go over to St Boan?'

The town where Uncle Adam and Aunt Lal lived was a seventy-minute train ride.

'Getting there should be okay. Coming back may be harder.'

'Well, at least snow can't last long in March,' Mum said.

Five minutes later a neighbour of

Aunt Lal rang to say he'd be driving through Abbot's Yarn in half an hour's time and could give me a lift. That would be quicker than the train which stopped at half a dozen tiny stations on its zig-zag journey.

'But I wish your new mail-order pyjamas had come,' said Mum.

'Aunt Lal won't mind holes in the elbows.'

In fact, while I was packing my toothbrush and well-worn pyjamas, a package arrived from Talland and Thermal Mail-wear, but it turned out to be only the Mystery Gift with a packer's note which said NIGHTWEAR TO FOLLOW.The Mystery Gift, when undone from layers of wrapping and an egg-sized box lined with cottonwool, proved to be a shiny new two-penny piece.

'Are they allowed to do that?' said Mum. 'Send money as a gift?'

'Shouldn't think so for a moment,' said Dad, who had just come home from fishing and was warming his frozen hands.

'I 'll keep it for luck,' I said and slid it down the inside pocket of my Perdidas jacket.

There was another knock at the door. This time it was Aunt Lal's neighbour. He said his name was Mark Hardisty.

'I hope you are ready,' he snapped. 'I don't want to lose any time.'

Luckily I was ready.

'It's very kind of you, Mr Hardisty,' Mum said doubtfully. I could see she didn't like him any more than I did. 'I do hope you get to St Boan before the bad weather sets in.'

'So do I. Throw your bag in the back and let's be off,' said Hardisty. I hardly had time to wave goodbye to Mum and Dad before he slammed the car into gear and roared off up the hill.

He was a lean, pale man with a big jaw full of teeth, and colourless eyes. He drove frighteningly fast. But I could understand why. A huge cliff of black cloud was climbing up the north-east sky behind us and the wind whistled past the car, even faster than we were going.

To distract myself from the way Mr Hardisty screeched round corners on two wheels, I tried to remember as much as I could about the Pernel twins.

They had been the children of a musician and composer, Carl Pernel, who had lived about a hundred years ago. He had written that famous tune, 'The Pilchard's Parade', which was sung and danced every year in St Boan at the August Festival. He was a native of St Boan and lived there all his life and had written a lot of other well-known music, 'A Cornish Symphony' and 'Atlantic Airs' and 'The Nine Maidens Cantata'. We learned about him at school He had played in all the capitals of Europe and his favourite violin was still to be seen in the St Boan Museum.

But the twins? His childen? There had been some mystery about them, I couldn't remember just what.

By now we had climbed out of Abbot's Yarn and were streaking along the high ridge road that runs a mile inland from all the little coast villages. The fields on each side are bony and bare, with rocks here and there, and groups of spooky white power-generating windmills, looking like Martians, now spinning madly in the gale, and here and there the granite tower of a deserted tin mine. It was a glum landscape, not made any more cheerful by the swarming snowflakes, like killer bees, that were pouring out of the black sky. I saw with relief the turn to Trenole Beach and knew that the St Boan road would be the next right.

'You certainly made good time, Mr Hardisty,' I said politely, hoping that he would slow down a bit, for the road narrowed here on a tricky right-hand bend known as Zawn Corner. But if anything he drove faster. Nothing could be seen ahead because of the seething snow.

And then suddenly – a pair of head-lights, dazzling through the murk, straight ahead. Hardisty stamped on his brake, the car spun like a billiard ball, and turned clean over. After a moment of crazy confusion I found myself dangling head down in my safety belt. To make matters worse, my face was in water.

I jerked my head back, managed to

reach for the knob of my belt, and undid myself. Hardisty was nowhere to be seen. The driver's door was half open and I supposed he had been thrown out. I couldn't get myself across the car and out of his door because the water was pouring through it – the car had landed slant-ways and upside down in a ditch. And I could feel that it was sinking.

On my side I couldn't escape because the door was jammed against the ditch bank. So I crept over my seat back, or under it, rather, into the back of the car. The rear seat had been folded flat to make more boot-space and the boot had been loaded with sacks of potatoes, which had split, and potatoes were bobbing about in the muddy water.

The prime question was could I open the boot door from inside?

At first I tried hammering and yelling

for help, but nobody answered.

Then I took a look at the lock, which was held in place by four screws.

If there was a tool-kit in the boot, with a screwdriver, it was not to be seen. It might be underneath the potatoes. Then again it might not. And the water level was rising quite fast.

At that point I remembered the Mystery Gift, the lucky two-penny piece I had tucked into my inside pocket.

It took me fifteen minutes to unscrew those four screws, using the lucky two-penny. When I pushed up the boot lid, water gushed in, and I just had time to scramble clear before the car filled up and sank down lower. I saw my night-bag floating among the spuds and grabbed it.

Next – with my heart in my mouth – I looked about for Hardisty. If he had been flung out he might be lying somewhere with broken bones, or a broken neck. But, strangely, there was no sign of him at all. Could he be under the water of the ditch? And where was the other car, whose lights directly ahead had caused Hardisty to skid?

With none of these questions answered I started the two-mile down-hill trudge into St Boan.

Up at the top was a new super-market, in process of building, and below it the big town school, the Hardisty School, built, I supposed, by an ancestor of my driver.

St Boan looked like a ghost town below me as I struggled down the hill through the snowstorm. It was packed tightly and steeply round a U-shaped harbour. The main road that I was on led straight to the quay. The snow-covered roofs of houses below me stuck up like sharks' teeth and the

harbour water beyond them was black.
A rough, gaping trench ran down one
side of the street, wide and deep
enough to drop a kitchen stove in, and
was protected by white-painted
trestles to stop people falling in, and
signs that said

NO CARS PERMITTED EXCEPT FOR
RESIDENTS' ACCESS

and

PEDESTRIANS PLEASE USE
OTHER WALKWAY.

Not a soul was about. I might have
been the only person in the place. No
doubt the natives were all at home by
their cosy fires. I saw nobody until I
crossed Queen Street, the main shop-
ping street of the town, where a
woman came tottering up to me on
the snow-covered slippery cobbles and
accosted me in a high, piercing voice.

'Hey there! You! Have you seen
two boys?'

I didn't like the way she spoke. There was something condescending about her voice, as if she only spoke to me because there was nobody else in the street.

But what right had she to be so haughty? She was a weird-looking scarecrow of a female, dressed as if for some party in a long draggly skirt of thin skimpy material. She had idiotically high-heeled shoes (considering the snow and the cobbles) and a kind of ostrich feather-scarf round her neck. Her lank, scanty hair, white, dyed yellow,blew about her face in elf-locks and her face was hollow-cheeked and haggard beyond belief. She looked like Noah's mother who had been left behind off the Ark and knew there was no use expecting help from anybody in this world

'Have you seen those two boys?' she demanded again angrily.

'No,' I said. 'No, I haven't seen anybody.'

She swung a thin leather strap in
her hand. It was a dog-lead, I noticed.

She said, 'Tell the boys their Aunt
Alida wants them right away. They
have got out – they have run off – tell
them!'

'But I haven't...'

She didn't wait to hear my answer,
but tottered away round a corner,
slipping on her high heels and with the
wind blowing her flimsy draperies.
Perhaps the storm had sent her wits
wandering, I thought. There were
flashes of greenish lightning through
the snow and every now and then a
snarl of thunder.

It was definitely not a night to be out
in freezing-wet clothes, and I was glad
when I came in sight of Uncle Adam's
cottage, which perched on a rocky
headland at the western edge of the

town.

For a moment, as I walked up to it, I thought there was a person in black standing by the door, waiting for me – then I realised that it was a young fir-tree, probably planted out there after Christmas.

I tapped on the door – a light showed inside – and went in.

CHAPTER TWO

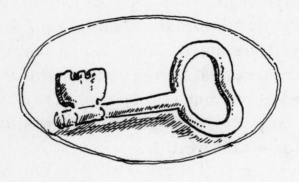

Some people think my Aunt Lal is an odd-looking woman. But she was not half so odd as the woman I had just met in the street. Aunt Lal has snow-white hair, worn flat and straight. Her nose is long and bony and usually rather pink because she suffers from hay-fever. Her eyes are blazing blue and see through you like laser beams. And she wears thick, heavy clothes bought at thrift shops. Nothing ever surprises or shocks her.

When I arrived, soaked, shivering, and speechless, she behaved as calmly as if I had just stepped off the Mailcoach Express. She had run a bath, phoned the local police, and fetched out some old clothes of Uncle Adam's before I had been in the house five minutes. And by the time a police inspector arrived to hear my tale, I was warm, dressed, and sitting by the fire drinking hot tea with a spoonful of Aunt Lal's walnut-leaf cordial in it.

'Well, Mrs Carne,' said Inspector Mutton. 'We've been up to Zawn Corner, that's a bad spot, that is. There've been plenty of crashes there – and we did find skid marks and indentations showing that a big vehicle had recently been overturned in the dyke, but,' he said, 'the vehicle itself had already been removed. Somebody must have got a breakdown service to the spot pretty smartly.'

'And there was nobody – no body – in the ditch?' I asked. 'You're sure of that?'

'Quite sure, young man.' The inspector glanced at me keenly. 'What was the name again – the name of the gentleman who gave you a lift?'

'Hardisty, Mark Hardisty. He said he was a neighbour of Aunt Lal.'

The Inspector and Aunt Lal exchanged an odd look. At least I thought it was odd. Then he said, 'Well – as no injury or fatality has been reported, we can take the matter no further at present. But I'll be in touch with you, Mrs Carne, directly, you may be sure, if anything should come up.'

And he left.

'It almost seemed as if he didn't believe me,' I suggested when the door had closed behind him.

'Oh no, he believed you,' Aunt Lal said thoughtfully. 'He believed you

all right.'

'How do you know that?'

'Because Hardisty is a local name. There are several in the town. And more in the graveyard.'

'Do you know a Mark?'

'Only in the graveyard.'

After a minute or two I said, 'What is the trouble about the Pernel twins?'

'Did you notice that half the streets in the town have been dug up? Deep trenches everywhere?'

'I certainly did!'

'They are laying new water pipes. The existing ones were put in a hundred years ago and they are corroded. And it is just about a hundred years ago,' said Aunt Lal, 'that the Pernel twins were lost. Their father had gone off to play in a concert in Plymouth. When he came home he found his house on fire, his brother and sister-in-law who lived there too were out at some meeting. He battled his way in to rescue the twins, but they were not in their beds. They were never seen again. The brother-in-law accused Pernel of leaving the boys to die. When he dashed into the burning building, all he brought out was a valuable violin. After that there was a lot of bad feeling in the town against Pernel.'

'What about the boys' mother? Where was she?'

'She had died when they were born. Her name was Lilian Hardisty. Her brother was Mark.'

'So,' I said slowly, 'perhaps he was the grandfather or great-grandfather of the man who gave me the lift.'

'Perhaps,' said Aunt Lal quietly.

After a moment she went on, 'When they dug up Fore Street to lay new waterpipes, they found two small skeletons on the site where Pernel's garden would have been. Their necks were broken. The house itself had been pulled down forty years before, when they widened Fore Street.'

'So perhaps the boys were dead before the house burned down?'

'The bones showed no sign of burning,' agreed Aunt Lal.

'What is the trouble in the town, Aunt Lal?' I asked. 'And why do you think I might be able to help?'

'The trouble,' she said. 'Ever since those bones were found, people keep seeing the ghosts of the twins. Sometimes on the shore, sometimes wandering along the street. Crying. It's as if being dug up disturbed something. A dozen times they've been seen in different places – by people you'd never expect to see a ghost, like Tom Pollard next door. Everybody in the town is getting jumpy and bad-tempered. They can hear the twins crying all the time. People say seeing the twins is a sign of bad luck. You know the Hellwethers and the Tollmen?'

I nodded. They were two clubs in the town who played a very wild, fierce game once a year trying to get a home-made football over a boundary line. Historians said that in the old days, before the Romans came to Cornwall for tin, the ball used had been a human head. Nowadays the two groups just had fights on street corners – if there was nothing better to do.

'They've taken sides about it,' said Aunt Lal. 'Some Pernel, some Hardisty.'

So – I wondered – why should I be expected to make sense of this spooky state of affairs? I hadn't even seen the twins, except in a dream. But, as if I had spoken aloud, Aunt Lal went on,

'It's because I had that dream about you and the twins – finding their music book.'

'Did I find it? In my dream they just asked for it.'

'You found it and gave it to them,' said Aunt Lal. 'And besides – you did help me before.'

A couple of years ago I had helped her get free from a kind of spell that had been laid on her. But at that time I myself had been helped by a strange boy called Eden, who had given me a key. I had met him on the train when visiting Aunt Lal. He told me he lived at Wicca Steps, farther along the coast, but Uncle Adam said there was no such place; it had fallen into the sea two hundred years ago. Since then I had had a few odd glimpses of Eden, as if he and I met on some different wavelength.

Remembering that, I looked up at my

Perdidas jacket, which Aunt Lal had hung on a coat-hanger from a hook in the mantelpiece. Absently, I stood up and rummaged in its pockets.

'I emptied them out,' said Aunt Lal. 'There was only a handkerchief and a two-penny piece. You'll find them on the shelf.'

'You missed this,' I said.

I pulled out a key. It was the one that Eden had given me. From time to time I lost it. But it always turned up again, as if it were part of some plan that was not yet complete.

'So what do you think I should do?' I said.

'We have to study what has happened to you,' she said. 'Somebody didn't want you to come here, that's plain. You will have to keep an eye out. They may try to stop you again.'

'Stop me?'

'Like by drowning you in a ditch,'

Aunt Lal said calmly. 'Let's think now – we might be able to get advice.'

'How?'

'One way is to switch on the radio and listen to the first thirteen words – I find that useful at times...'

She pressed the radio button and at once a voice said, 'Woe unto you, lawyers! For ye have taken away the key of knowledge.'

The door opened and Uncle Adam came in with Nibs the cat, who went everywhere with him. They were both coated with snow.

'It's coming down like mashed potato,' said Uncle Adam. 'I think we may have Ned with us for quite a while.'

CHAPTER THREE

After Uncle Adam had made fragrant
fish soup for supper (he always did the
cooking, Aunt Lal was quite useless in
that department) and we had all eaten
the soup, including Nibs, I went to
bed. I was dead tired. And my own
clothes would not be dry till morning.

I went to sleep at once. And, helter-
skelter, as if I'd stepped on to a
moving walkway, I began to dream.

The twins were there, Mat and Ben.
Mat was the one who thought he was a

dog and ran around on all fours. His brother was very patient with him.

'It was their Aunt Alida's fault,' the boy who lived next door to the twins told me. 'After she came to look after the twins, she used to punish Mat by making him go in the dog kennel, out in the back garden. If you treat a person like a dog, they'll end up acting like one.'

'Why was their aunt in charge of them?'

'She and her brother came when their sister died. Pernel was rich, he had a big house, he was famous already. So they moved in. He was often abroad, playing in concerts. Mark and Alida treated the boys badly. I used to see them crying in the garden.'

'Aren't you Eden? Who gave me the key? Why did you live next door to the Pernels? I thought you were miles away along the coast in Wicca Steps?'

'That was before we moved,' he said.
'The twins were a lot younger than me.
They used to be sent out even when it
was bitter cold. Their uncle stuck the
dog kennel up in the big cherry tree
and told them to take shelter in that
if they were chilly. If I went to play
with them he threw stones at me and
told me to get back over the fence.
Mind you don't lose that key I gave
you. You'll need to use it at least twice
more.'

'How can I help the twins?'

'They want their father. And he
wants them. But they are lost.'

Mat and Ben were running along the
street. Ben was howling miserably, and
Mat was calling out, 'Dad? Dad? Where
are you, Dad?' in a thin hopeless voice.

Their Uncle Mark came out and
furiously dragged them back indoors. I
saw him aim a kick at Ben, who let out
a yelp. I saw that he was the man who

had given me the lift. He had not
drowned in the ditch, it seemed.

'What can I do?' I asked Eden.

'You can help the boys by remembering the tune their dad wrote for
them,' Eden told me.

'What tune?'

He whistled a lively quick scatter of
notes, and then sang:

'This is the song
Of Mat and Ben
It rattles along
Without where or when
Oh, when, oh, where, oh, where or
when
Will the poor twins find their dad
again?'

A skinny lady came walking along
the street. She carried an umbrella
with ribbons tied to the handle and
aimed a whack with it at Eden, who
slipped through the door.

'Don't lose the key!' he called to me.

'Don't forget the tune! It's in the key of D!'

The tune was very like one I had made up for singing in the bath when I was a lot younger:

'My bath is as wide as the Bristol
Channel,
I've lost the soap,
I've lost the flannel...'

I'll easily be able to remember it, I thought. The last thing I remembered was Aunt Alida saying, 'Stop singing that vulgar tune!'

Then I woke up and found that the cat Nibs was sitting on my chest and trying to open my eyes by gently dabbing them with his paw, which was a habit he had when bored by his own company and eager for breakfast.

CHAPTER FOUR

The scene outside my bedroom window was white and silent. Snow had stopped falling, but the sky was still heavy with it. The only sound came from the grey-and-white sea, lurching and slapping against the rocks of the point.

I went downstairs, and found my clothes which had dried overnight. Adam and Lal were still asleep, so I fed Nibs, ate a piece of bread and marmalade, and went out into the hushed, empty world. Nibs took one look at it and turned back indoors. I walked down to the point and watched the waves tipping to and fro and the white gulls rocking on them, staring at me haughtily with their pale cold eyes, as if they knew a secret that I didn't. They were like Mark Hardisty and his sister, I thought, with their mean expressions and curved cruel beaks.

The terrible thing was that I had forgotten the tune. In my dream the notes that Eden whistled had come through quite clear and plain – it was a quick, catchy tune. I had felt quite sure of remembering it – but now it was clean gone, the corner inside my head where bits of music were stored and brought out when wanted felt like an empty dustbin. I could remember 'God Save the Queen', I could remember 'Ten Green Bottles' but 'This is the

Song of Mat and Ben' was null and void as the dinosaur or the dodo. I couldn't even think of my own tune that was similar to the one I wanted – sometimes you can rescue an escaped tune that way, by starting off with something that has a similar pattern of notes; but no – this one had gone right out of reach, into hollow nowhere.

I had been straining my ears – the way you do when you are trying to fetch a tune out from where it is hiding – and now I caught the sound of voices fiercely shouting. The noise came from the direction of the main quay, so I walked that way, to see what was going on.

My fingers found the key in my pocket and I thought, later I must go and hunt through the books in Adam's shop, perhaps there really is an old music book there that once belonged to the twins, with the tune in it – but the shop will be locked up at this time of the morning. Then I turned a corner, by a pub called *The Hornpipe Cat* – The sign showed a cat dancing on hind legs – and came out on to the Town Quay. This was a wide flat space at the head of the harbour, with the lifeboat in its shed at the top of a ramp on one side and the harbourmaster's office on the other.

In the middle two groups were hurling snowballs at each other. One lot wore red caps, the other had blue. Some of them were shrilly whistling tunes.

The fight may have started in a friendly way, but I could see that it was turning nasty. Stones were being loaded into the snowballs, I caught a glint of knives and knuckledusters, there were splashes of blood on the snow. A policeman over on the far side of the harbour had loudly blown his

whistle and was now talking urgently into his mobile phone.

Stay away from trouble, Aunt Lal had said. There was absolutely no sense in getting mixed up in a rough-house between the Hellwethers and the Tollmen – and I was about to turn and go back the way I had come when a rock-loaded snowball smacked me on the side of my head and I passed out cold. Next thing I knew I was being dragged towards the jetty and voices were shouting:

'Toss him overboard! Dump him in the briny! Who needs his rotten tunes? Chuck him in! Murderer! Child killer! Did in his own kids!'

I began to protest and struggle. 'Let me go! Leave me alone! I'm not a murderer...' and suddenly found that I was looking up into the faces of Inspector Mutton and a policeman in a helmet.

'It's all right, it's all right, keep calm. Take it easy! No one's calling you a murderer!' they were saying.

I felt a fool.

I sat up and saw that I was nowhere near the harbourside. I was in fact still outside *The Hornpipe Cat*; and the two policemen hoisted me up and took me into it and bought me a cup of hot chocolate.

'You were only knocked out for a moment – Dan here saw you cop one, and drop, so he came and helped you up.'

I apologized confusedly. 'I thought they were dragging me across the quay and were going to drop me into the harbour.'

'You took quite a bash on the head. You'll have a black eye tomorrow, likely.'

'Best go home to your aunt for now.'

'What happened to them – all the

chaps who were fighting?'

'Oh, they run off, soon's I blow my whistle. We know them! Hellwethers and Tollmen. Happen we'll run a few in, time they start another of their scrummages.' Dan grinned at me and said, 'Your aunt'll want to put a bit of beefsteak on that eye.'

'I'll walk you back there,' Inspector Mutton said. And he did so. I felt even more of a fool. Here I was, invited to St Boan to put right trouble in the town, and as soon as I stepped out of doors, had to be escorted home like a child.

But Aunt Lal took it with her usual calm. She inspected my bruised forehead, wrapped a bit of snow in a handkerchief, and said, 'Hold that there for half an hour and I don't think it will be much.'

When Inspector Mutton had left, I asked Aunt Lal: 'What happened to Carl Pernel? After his house burned down?'

Suddenly she looked very tired. She said, 'That is the worst part of the story. People in the town accused him of leaving his children to die in the burning house. So one day an angry mob chased him and stoned him and threw him into the harbour. His head hit a rock and he drowned.'

'That was it,' I said slowly. 'That's what I was remembering. After the stone hit me.'

'You hooked on to his mind for a moment. Poor man,' Aunt Lal said.

'You said he was a rich man. What happened to his money after he died?'

'It went to Mark and Alida Hardisty – his wife's brother and sister. They rebuilt the house and lived there. And with some of the money they endowed a school. There's a big memorial to them in the church, and a big tombstone in the graveyard.'

'Nobody ever suggested that they might have done away with the twins?'

'No. But they came to a queer end.'

'Why? What happened to them?'

'You know the cliff path runs west-ward from here, all the way along the coast to Land's End. And before you get to the ruins of Croopus Castle there is Cold Point where the land runs out, and there's a flattish bit of ground which is quite dangerous because of a deep hole going down to a tin mine that's all worked out. Five years ago they built a shed round the hole with signs saying DANGER, but back in those days that wasn't so. Well, one night a man called Rumpot Roche (because of the amount of liquor he used to put away) was walking home along the cliff path from visiting his lady-friend at St Clew, and he looked down and saw the Hardistys. The cliff path does some zig-zagging there, and they were down below him on a lower bend. It was a summer evening, not full dark, and he could easily recognise them because of the black suit Hardisty always wore and a kind of ostrich-feather tippet Alida had round her neck...'

'Yes,' I said. 'And she carried an umbrella.'

'The queer thing, Roche thought, was that they were being led. Two little lights went on ahead of them flickering like candle-flames. He couldn't see who or what was carrying them, but they were low down, at knee height. Then, when they got to where the deep hole was, they all vanished, the Hardisty couple and the lights too. Next day Mark and Alida were found at the bottom of the hole with broken necks. It was the day they were supposed to open the new school.'

'So all of them died,' I said. 'Everyone

in the story. Pernel and the twins and Mark and Alida. Is Pernel buried in the churchyard too?'

'Yes. They put up a stone to him with his name and history, but people kept defacing it and writing 'Murderer' so now there is just a simple slab with his initials. One rector said there should be a tablet in the church. Pernel was one of the town's most famous inhabitants, but other people said no, look what he was accused of doing. So nothing was done.'

'It's a bit sad.'

'Yes.'

Uncle Adam came downstairs. 'Hullo,' he said, 'been in the wars? Do you want to come along to the shop and look for a book?'

'Yes, please,' I said.

On the way to the shop Uncle Adam asked me, 'Seen the twins yet, have you?'

'Only in dreams. Not while I was awake. Have you seen them, Uncle Adam?'

'No, I haven't. But lots in the town have. And nobody likes it. Think they're going to come down with meningitis or Mad Cow Disease as a result of seeing the boys. Stupid. But that's how people are. My helper in the shop, Mrs Fearon, she's seen the twins several times around the town and she won't come to the shop any more. Says she'd drop dead of fright if they walked in the door. So your aunt is quite right. Something's got to be done about them.'

'Well, I wish I could see them.'

'Maybe you will by and by,' he said encouragingly.

CHAPTER FIVE

Uncle Adam's shop was very dusty. I
supposed that was due to Mrs Fearon's
absence.

I started on the top shelves, taking
out each book in turn, leafing through
it, shaking it to make sure nothing was
tucked between the pages. After a
couple of hours I had gone through
one set of shelves and found nothing at
all. Adam and I were both coughing
and sneezing from all the dust I had

dislodged. When we went home at lunchtime he said, 'You'd better take a walk this afternoon, young Ned, and get some fresh air into your lungs.'

'Why not visit the museum,' Aunt Lal said. 'They've got Pernel's manuscripts there, and one of his instruments.'

I'm not crazy about museums. I've seen too many dusty old pots and rusty old billhooks on school expeditions. I thought I would go to the graveyard first. St Boan graveyard is on a steep bit of hillside, practically one-in-three up above the town. A path leads directly to it from Uncle Adam's house. So up it I went, and soon had a fine view of all the snow-capped headlands along the coast, and the slate-coloured sea, white and frothy at the edges, tossing against cliffs.

The graveyard was full of Hardistys and Trelawnys and Treffrys and

Pengellys. And a big handsome granite memorial to Mark and Alida Hardisty, founders of the Hardisty School.

At last, right up at the top, I found a single stone, no bigger than a milestone, with C.P. on it and his dates. Most of the other graves had bunches of snowdrops and daffodils and greenhouse hyacinths, now half-covered in snow, but this one had nothing. And somebody had hacked away half the lettering with a chisel. And somebody else had dumped some garbage beside the stone. It would be easy to do this, for the grave was just within the boundary wall, and a road ran on the other side.

I felt sorry for Pernel. Poor man, what had he done to deserve all this hate and scorn? Only saved his precious instrument, which was the mainstay of his living. And he had searched for the twins first. I wondered what Pernel had looked like. I had a clear notion of Mark and Alida, the unkind brother and sister, and of the twins, queer little brats, – but nobody had given me a description of Pernel himself. As I stood thinking this, a boy shot past me on a bike, on the other side of the wall. He was whistling a very familiar tune – I just caught a snatch of it, and then he was gone and the tune with him...

The boy had the look of my ghost friend, Eden. Sometimes I don't see Eden for months. And then he will turn up in a dream, or a glimpse in a crowd. Sometimes he gives me good advice.

Mist was rising all around and the boy and the bike disappeared into it.

Then I noticed something odd. A lot of the tombstones in this part of the graveyard had plainly been made by the same stonemason, who had a fond-

Here lies
the mortal remains
of
WILLIAM TRELAWN

born 1st May 1702

R.I.P.

ness for a stone with a curved top decorated by a pair of plump cherubs sitting at ease on the lower end of the curve. Now – out of the corner of my eye – I thought I saw two of those cherubs jump nimbly down off a headstone and scamper away downhill into the mist. I gave my head a bit of a shake and stared hard – but they were gone, out of sight. They must have been a couple of gulls, I decided, which would be about the same size.

I tramped down through the snow to the museum, which occupied what used to be a warehouse on the harbourside.

The museum was a pleasant surprise, as there were no dusty pots or rusty billhooks. All the contents were elegantly displayed in glass cases with bright lighting and photographs of tin mines and half-size models of fishing boats. I asked at the desk if they had a portrait of Carl Pernel, and was sent upstairs to the music department and given a pair of head-phones which would provide me with a commentary about the exhibits.

Just as I reached the top of the stairs I heard a crash of glass break-ing, and a woman's voice cry out in alarm. I walked through a doorway into the music department to find the floor sparkling with glass splinters and fragments of varnished wood.

'Did you do that?' bawled a red-faced woman to me.

'Do what?'

'Throw that pot!'

'I haven't thrown any pot,' I said, utterly mystified.

Then I saw that one of the big glass cases had been completely smashed, along with its contents. A label on the floor by my foot said, FAVOURITE GUARNERI VIOLIN OF CARL PERNEL.

A large broken clay pot lay among the debris – just the kind I don't like.

'You must have thrown it,' declared the woman furiously. 'You were just outside the door and the pot came through it.'

'Well, I didn't.'

'No, he didn't,' said a girl, one of the museum staff, who had come up behind me to lead me to the portrait of Carl Pernel. 'I was close behind him all the way up, and he hadn't any pot.'

'Where did it come from then? He must have thrown it! Send for the police!'

The police were sent for, and turned out to be the familiar Inspector Mutton.

'Trouble seems to follow you around, my lad,' he said to me. But the curator girl, Rose Killigrew, held by her story that I couldn't possibly have thrown any pot, for she had been within

touching distance of me all the way
from the ground floor.

'Well, it's a downright disgrace, whoever did it!' said the furious woman.
'Pernel's violin smashed and his
portrait damaged too – it was knocked
right off the wall.'

While they were discussing the
damage and the insurance, and
whether the wrecked violin could ever
be mended, and while Inspector
Mutton was taking notes, I studied
the portrait and was astonished.

Pernel was so young!

I had always thought of him as being
an elderly character, in his forties or
fifties perhaps – but this man looked
no more than twenty-five. He had a
thatch of brownish fair hair and freck-
les, like the twins, and was smiling a
shy half-smile as he looked down at a
fiddle-bow that he held in his hands.
It wasn't a very good painting – done

by a local amateur – but it made him seem like a person, a real person. And pitifully young to have had all those tragic things happen to him. As soon as I saw the picture of him I thought, he would never run out of a blazing house and leave two children to burn to death. No way!

Thinking these things I absently fitted the headphones over my ears – and loudly into them lilted and sang the music of Pernel's tune for his sons, 'This is the song of Mat and Ben...'

Turning round I was just in time to see two small boys in rusty black suits scamper away from me and slither down the stairs.

'Oh, stop them!' I gasped. 'Stop those boys! Wait, won't you?'

But nobody else had seen them, it seemed, and they were gone long before I got down to the ground floor.

I ran back upstairs, frantically

clutching the tune in my head, like a
live, wriggling fish, and asked Rose
Killigrew if there were any manuscripts
of Pernel's music in the museum. Yes,
several, she told me, and I whistled her
the tune and asked if she knew that
one. But she shook her head. She was
a music expert, and she had cata-
logued all the Pernel documents they
had. She was quite sure that particular
melody was not among them.

'It's such a lively, distinctive tune,
isn't it,' she said. 'Whistle it again!'

And of course – when I tried – it was
clean gone.

'But it was on tape, on the head-
phones,' I said. 'That's how I caught it
again!'

Rose shook her head. 'I've never
heard that tune before,' she said. 'I'm
sure it isn't recorded on the headphone
tape.'

She was right. When we played the

headphone tape right through, it was not there.

I went out, heavy with sadness and frustration.

I would have liked to sit on a bench and watch the gulls swooping and look at the harbour, which was full of slopping, chopping green water for the tide had come up high, and try my

hardest to remember the tune.

But all the benches were covered a hand's depth in snow, so I went home to Aunt Lal instead.

She listened to my story with close attention.

'It's bound to be the Hardistys – it must be their malice and ill-will that is trying to prevent you from helping those twins,' she said. 'But you seem to be getting closer to them. At least you saw them.'

'I think it helps me to see them when I hear the tune,' I said. 'It seems to fetch them.'

Mrs Fearon dropped in just then for a cup of tea. She was a fat, comfort-able body whose natural expression should have been cheerful. But she looked worried and upset.

'It is so distressing,' she said. 'I never could abide the sound of kids crying – when it was my own I always had to pick them up straightaway. Tom used to say I spoiled ours rotten. And now to hear that grizzling and boohooing going on all the time, nighttime and daytime too – it's more than a body can bear!'

She glared at Aunt Lal as if it were her fault.

'I know,' said Aunt Lal. 'They want their father, poor dears. The puzzle of it is, why doesn't he hear them? Everybody else seems to.'

'I don't,' I said. 'Except in dreams.'

'It's getting everybody down,' Mrs Fearon went on. 'The adults are all tired and snappish and the kids quarrel...trade's bad, tourists aren't coming...'

'That's partly because all the streets are dug up,' Aunt Lal pointed out.

'It's because the shopkeepers are ratty and unhelpful, too. And those mobs of Tollmen and Hellwethers scrapping and skirmishing all over the streets! Why can't they go and fight each other up on the moor?'

'There's more ammunition for them in the town,' Aunt Lal suggested. 'Stones and cobbles all ready dug up by the Water Board lying handy for use. Which reminds me, how is your black eye coming, Ned?'

'It's nothing much,' I said.

'Talking about things dug up by the Water Board,' Mrs Fearon said, 'my hubby found a thing this morning he thought Mr Carne would like to look at...'

Aunt Lal's mention of my bruise had reminded me of how I was knocked flat on the quay, and mechanically I stuck my hands in my pockets to check that the key and the lucky two-penny piece were safe.

They were not there.

I must go back, I thought at once. At

once! To the spot outside *The
Hornpipe Cat* where I was knocked
down. That's where they will be. Might
be. In the snow.

'My hubby has a job with the Water
Board, you know,' Mrs Fearon was
clacking on, 'the pay's not wonderful,
what is, these days? His men dug up
this box in one of the side-cuts they
took off the main trench in Fore Street
– kind of a tin box, lawyers' box he
thought it might be, all caked over with
rust and muck, maybe got papers
inside it – thought Mr Carne would be
interested...'

'A box full of papers...?' Aunt Lal
was beginning eagerly, when there was
a knock at the door.

It was Inspector Mutton. 'You lost a
key?' he said to me.

'Yes. Yes!'

'Ah! Thought it might be yours.
Found in the snow, it was, outside

The Hornpipe Cat. It's down at the station, you want to go and claim it.'

'Thank you very much,' I said. 'I'll go directly.'

But now Uncle Adam came home, clasping carefully in his arms an amazing, crusted earthy, rusty object about the size of a small backpack with no particular shape.

'Spread out some newspaper would you, lovey,' he said to Aunt Lal, who did so in front of the hearth.

'That's the thing my hubby found in the trench,' Mrs Fearon said proudly. 'Did you ever see anything so filthy? I wouldn't want it on my hearthrug, I can tell you – covered in germs, I daresay – eh, well, best be getting back to make the old man's tea, he's grumpy enough as it is...'

I was torn. I wanted to race down to the police station and pick up my key without loss of time; on the other

hand I was ragingly curious about the
thing Mr Fearon had found.

Uncle Adam had scraped all the
loose earth off it using a brush and
dustpan. Now, with a chisel and a
plasterer's trowel, he was scraping
away at the rust.

'It seems to be a metal chest with a
handle on top,' he said. 'Like those
Japanned deed boxes lawyers used to
keep wills and documents in. Pass me
the oil, will you, Ned; and a steel wool
pad, and a skewer. Yes: under the
handle I think I can see what might be
a keyhole!'

A keyhole!

'Where's the police station, Aunt
Lal?' I said. 'I've got to go and pick up
my key. I've a feeling –'

'That your key might fit the lock?
You never know!' she said. 'The police
station is just off the harbour front, in
that narrow lane – Tucking Street –

behind the harbourmaster's office.
Only five minues from here. But run –
the snow has started again. Here, wear
this cap.' She crammed a blue knitted
cap on my head.

'They'll think he's one of the
Tollmen,' grunted Uncle Adam, on his
knees, scrubbing away.

'Rubbish! But hurry, Ned.'

CHAPTER SIX

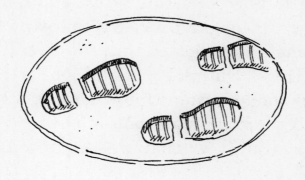

I ran all the way to the police station.
And ahead of me, in the snowy dusk, I
thought I could almost see two little
figures scooting along. And as I ran,
my feet thudding and scrunching on
the new snow, I could almost remember the tune:

'This – is – the – song – of – Mat
– and – Ben –'

My bath is as wide as the Bristol
Channel...

At the police station they had a phoned message from Inspector Mutton and were quite ready to hand over the key and the two-penny piece to me if I confirmed that they were mine, which I did.

Outside it was by now almost dark, and the snow was coming down so hard that it was like walking through a forest.

I started back the way I had come, but before I had taken half a dozen steps, someone grabbed me from behind – hands clenched on my elbows, two people, I thought – the woolly cap was pulled down hard over my face so that I couldn't see, and I was forced forward at a headlong pace. My arms were clamped ferociously behind my back. Whoever was thrusting me onward had twice my strength, and I could only just breathe because of the thick fabric muffling my

nose and mouth. I stumbled along
half-fainting, half-choking, unable to
shout for help.

It was like a nightmare. But it was
real. And it went on for too long, for
what seemed endless time, but was, I
suppose, ten to fifteen minutes –
tripping, half-falling, struggling over a
rough, snowy, rocky surface.

Then I was flung down, violently, on
the ground, and I suppose did pass
out, as I had before on the
harbourside. This time for longer.

When I came round I found myself
in complete pitch dark, and I was
stupid and dazed with cold. For a
while I thought that my hands were
tied behind my back and then slowly
realised that they were not tied, but
just numb and dead, half frozen from
being lain on. I pulled myself up
shakily, shoved my hands under my
chin, inside my jacket, blew on them,

tucked them under my arms, and, after a while, gradually a bit of feeling began to come back into them.

I thought, I must get up, get away from here, or I shall die of cold. But where is here? The ache in my hands and feet was unbearable, I knew that if I didn't move, walk, jump, get into motion somehow, I might very easily die, as people do on mountains, in avalanches...

If only my mind would function and help me – but that seemed as frozen and paralysed as every other part of me... Now I remembered being shoved along, at a stumbling run, from the police station, but who had done it? Was it Hellwethers or Tollmen or – a more frightening thought – was it Mark Hardisty and his sister, revisiting St Boan from whatever unrestful unhappy region they now occupied – come back to prevent Carl Pernel from ever finding his children?

As my mind began sluggishly to move, I could feel the circulation creeping back to my hands and feet.

Agony, it was. I stretched out my arms and felt around me to find out whether, by touch, I could learn anything about my surroundings. Was I in a cave, a tomb, a cell, a cellar?

One hand touched rough, splintery planking. So I was in a wooden building, it seemed. But where? I thought we had come some way from the town. And I could hear wind, overhead and all around, besides the distant, regular boom of waves breaking not far off. I must be above ground, then. At first I had been afraid that I was down a mine, somewhere underground. But the sounds of wind and waves were comforting, in a way.

Then an even more frightening thought came to me. Mark and Alida

Hardisty had fallen down a mine hole. I remembered Aunt Lal saying that it was on Cold Point. It used to be uncovered, but they've put a shed over it now.

Could I be in that shed? A shed built around a large, deep hole?

Shakily, groggily, propping myself against the wall that I could feel with my right hand, I pulled myself up till I was standing. Then I began to move forward very slowly, testing the ground with each foot in turn before I put my weight on it.

After about four steps I came to a corner, an angle in the wall.

Then – terrifyingly – when I felt ahead with my left foot, I found nothing. The ground was not there. It was like arriving at a step down, a deep step. How deep I had no means of telling. With extreme caution, I turned myself around and began inching along in the other direction. This way, the wall went on farther – about a dozen steps. Then another corner. Then I felt a post, or joist, an interruption in the wall and a crack in the planking. A door! With painstaking care I fingered the door, up first, as far as I could reach, then down to ground level.

I found two hinges. So the handle, or latch, must be on the other side. Plank by plank I felt my way across that door as if I were an archaeologist working on an inscription.

Finally I came to a latch and a keyhole.

A keyhole!

I lifted the latch, pushed the door – pulled it as hard as I could – but it didn't budge, either way. Locked.

No one but a crazy fool would expect the key I had picked up from the police to fit this keyhole – nevertheless I tried

it. And it did fit. The door opened
outwards. I edged through, removed
the key, and stuffed it back in my
pocket. Shut the door again behind
me. And stepped out on to rough,
tussocky, snowy ground, with wind
scouring my face and snow flinging
itself against my eyes and mouth.

Which way to go?

East, it must be. Cold Point, where
the wooden shed covered a pit-shaft,
where the two Hardistys had been
found with broken necks, lay to the
west of St Boan. Therefore, all I had to
do was face into the icy wind and keep
going.

Easier said than done.

Outside the shed, though, it was just
fractionally lighter than inside. I could
see the rocky outline of the headland
and the sea, a pale gleam, down below,
and the white breakers curving in on
the town beach, ahead, and the West

Pier sticking out, like a black finger above them, into the sea. But the cliff path was narrow and rough, and if I should chance to slip there was nothing much to break my fall on to rocks below. And the wind beat and battered against me, making it hard to go forward steadily, pushing me off balance.

Oddly enough, what I felt most was lonely.

If only I had someone to talk to.

The thought that at least twenty minutes of this slow, staggering progress lay ahead of me before I reached the town was so daunting that half a dozen times I was on the point of just slumping down in a tussock of snowy heather and giving up.

But then, through the whine of the wind, I felt I was listening to a voice that said:

I was lonely too. Keep going.

You were lonely.

Very lonely. Everybody hated me.
When I walked out of doors people's
faces were cold and ugly with hate and
scorn. Because they said I had let my
children die.

But couldn't you tell them that was
not true?

They refused to believe me. Because,
where were the children? They said I
cared for nothing but my music. They
made me into an outcast.

How terrible.

Yes, it was terrible. But you can help
me now.

How?

Find the boys. Tell them that I am
waiting for them. That, once we are
together, nothing will matter.

How can I find them?

Sing. Sing my song. Then they will
hear, then they will know who sent
you, where you come from.

But how can I remember the song?

Listen to the wind, the wind in the key of D. The key, the key...

His light, cold hand caught hold of mine, and all the way along the cliff path he led me – steadily, safely, against knifing wind, against cutting snow – while his music threaded the howl of the gale and made the walk ahead seem within my power.

When the lights of the town began to prickle out dimly through the snow and vapour, Pernel's faint cold grasp melted away. He was gone, and the music was gone too. With all my strength I tried to keep the tune in my head, but it melted like snowflakes...

CHAPTER SEVEN

Inspector Mutton was at Uncle Adam's house when I got back.

'Where have you been? What happened to you?' they all shouted at me. They sounded angry, not welcoming. But then Aunt Lal, seeing the state I was in, relented and took me off to the kitchen for a drink of hot milk and ginger and a rub-down.

She told how anxious they had grown when after twenty minutes, after forty minutes, I had not come back, and how Uncle Adam had rung the police who said I had been in and out of the office in five minutes. A search had been started, but the weather conditions were so bad that it was a fairly hopeless task.

'What happened to you, Ned?' she asked again when my teeth had stopped chattering.

I explained, as well as I was able. I had picked up the key and then been abducted.

'It must have been Mark and Alida,' she said positively. 'Taking you to the spot where their own lives ended. Hoping to finish you off in the same way.'

'Why didn't they push me down the hole?'

'Perhaps he stopped them.'

'Carl?'

'Yes.'

I thought about my companion on the way home. I had not told her about that. I asked, 'Has Uncle Adam managed to open the box?'

'Not yet. He found the keyhole, but it was all caked up with rust. So he dribbled in a bit of oil and left it to soften the blockage. It should be worth trying by now.'

We went back to the front room. Inspector Mutton had gone, leaving a message for me to present myself at the police station tomorrow morning to give an account of what had happened to me.

Uncle Adam was dozing with Nibs on his knee, but he opened his eyes the minute we came in and said. 'Did you get that key?'

I pulled it out of my pocket, thinking how unlikely it was that the same key would open the door of a shed and the lid of a lawyer's deed box. But still it seemed the right size for the keyhole.

'You try it,' said Uncle Adam, when he had scooped and scrabbled in the keyhole with the quill of a gull's feather and carefully scraped out some sludge of oily rust.

I slid the key into the hole. It went in, slowly and grittily. I tried to turn it. But it stuck fast.

Adam tried. Lal tried. None of us could turn it.

'I wonder if I used pliers,' Adam pondered.

'No!' cried Lal. 'You might break the key.'

'What then?'

'I'll try the radio,' she said.

'Radio!'

But she switched on, saying, 'Anyway it's time for my favourite programme, "Mislaid Melodies" – listen –'

And what came on was the twins' tune. My fingers were on the key at that moment, I gripped it and turned steadily. At the end of the short piece of music the announcer said, 'Nobody knows where that tune came from. Perhaps it is the national anthem of Never Never Land. That was a very ancient recording, played on Mozart's harmonica, recorded on an early phonograph towards the end of the last century –'

The key finished its turn and I could hear the lock click.

Uncle Adam pulled up the lid, which resisted, but then came creakily open. The box was filled with yellow wrinkled documents, slightly crumpled at the edges, tied in flat packs with faded red ribbon. The top one was embossed with a red seal and inscribed in large gothic lettering: LAST WILL AND TESTAMENT OF CARL FRANCIS PERNEL.

Uncle Adam opened it and read:

'This is the last Will and Testament

of me, Carl Francis Pernel, being of sound mind and good health on this 27th day of April 1898. In hopes that my beloved sons Matthew and Benjamin may yet be found live and well, I bequeath all my worldly goods to them. And I hereby revoke my previous Will leaving money to my brother-in-law and sister-in-law Mark and Alida Hardisty. I leave them nothing. And, if the twins are never found, my fortune shall go to endow a school of music to teach poor boys who could not otherwise afford lessons.'

'Well,' said Aunt Lal, 'the twins have been found – at least their bones – so now what will happen to the money? If there is any left?'

'Lawyers will have to argue about that,' said Uncle Adam. 'Probably most of it was spent on establishing the Hardisty School.'

He lifted out some other documents

which he said were the title-deeds of
Pernel's house that had been pulled
down. Then he came to a flat book
with handsomely marbled covers. It
was like a very grand school exercise-
book. And it was labelled:

A NOTEBOOK
OF TUNES AND SONGS FOR MY
LITTLE SONS MAT AND BEN.

Inside, the very first tune, in the key
of D, written in ink, was the one I had
been trying so hard to capture, with
the words written underneath:

'This is the song of Mat and Ben
This is the song of Ben and Mat
It bounds away like an acrobat
This is the song of Mat and Ben
It rattles along without where
or when
But yet some day the search will
be ended
The lost ones found and the
trouble mended

The seekers come to the end
of the quest
The hurts be healed and the
weary rest.'

Aunt Lal said, 'Adam, why don't
you get your accordion and we'll go out
and play that music in the street.'

'In this weather? At this time of
night? Are you mad, woman?'

'No, look,' she said. 'It has stopped
snowing. The moon has come out. It
would be the right thing to do.'

'Oh, very well.'

'Ned and I will sing the words. And –
and perhaps people will hear and come
out and join in. Wrap this muffler
round your neck' she said to me.
'Where is the cap I gave you?'

'It might be on Cold Point.'

'Lucky I have several.'

Adam fetched his accordion – a very
old one which came from Vienna over a
hundred years ago – and wrapped like

Eskimos, we stepped out into the blazing moonlight. The newly fallen snow was already crisp with frost and the white surfaces gleamed and flashed.

The harmonica's loud joyful music fetched echoes from every corner. Lal and I both sang as loudly as we could.

Windows began to shoot open and heads popped out. Then doors began to open. People emerged to find out what on earth was going on. The hour was not late after all – no more than half-past nine. It was the weather that had kept everybody indoors. But now, tempted out by brilliant moonlight and irresistible music, householders and their children came bustling out again. The narrow streets filled up with singing, dancing neighbours.

Uncle Adam led the serpentine trail of singers and dancers twice around the town, up Fore Street and down Church Street, then out on to the

harbour front.

'This is the song of Mat and Ben
Of Ben and Mat, of Mat and Ben
Oh when oh where, oh where or when
Will those twins find their dad again?'

Just for about twenty seconds I saw two little capering figures dart across the quay and greet a fair-haired young man who came climbing up the harbour steps to greet them and throw his arms round them. Then a mass of people swept across the cobbles and blotted out my view.

Rose Killigrew from the museum, arriving beside me, said, 'So you managed to find the manuscript with that tune after all!'

'Yes,' I told her. 'It's in a book that Carl Pernel made for the twins. I'll bring it round to you tomorrow. And there's a lot of legal documents too. Maybe the Hardisty School will have to close down.'

A boy who was bounding along on my other side said, 'Their Uncle Mark murdered them. He cut through the branch that supported their dog-kennel in the cherry tree. So the branch gave way when they climbed inside the kennel. They fell and broke their necks. And he buried them in the garden.'

'Eden! Why didn't you tell me that before?'

'You had to find the book first. You had to learn the tune,'

'That key of yours?'

'Keep it,' he said. 'You haven't finished with it yet. You'll be wanting it again.'

Then he jogged away behind some dancing Tollmen and I lost sight of him.

Inspector Mutton said to Uncle Adam, 'I ought to arrest you for creating a breach of the peace. But

nobody seems to be doing any harm.
So we'll let it go.'

The people went on dancing until
sunrise.

Next day the snow melted as fast as it
had come and I was able to go home
by train.

Aunt Lal's blue cap was found in the
shed on Cold Point beside the twenty-
metre-deep hole where the Hardistys
had fallen to their death.

Aunt Lal phoned some days after I
got home to tell me that the town
council was changing the name of the
Hardisty School to the Carl Pernel
School, and there would be a big
music department.

She said, 'They are going to put up a
memorial tablet in the church to Carl
Francis Pernel, famous musician and
composer of this town, and his twin
sons, Matthew and Benjamin. And

they are going to bury the twins' bones in the graveyard and put up a gravestone beside their father's. You had better come over for the ceremony.'

'If you don't want me before that,' I said.

For when I got home, Mum told me, 'Your friend Eden rang up. Which one is he? Do I know him? He said he'd soon have another job for you. What did he mean by that? What kind of job?'

I fingered the key in my pocket.

'Opening something, I suppose.'